À mon papa, Ken le géant costaud courageux, qui n'a peur
de rien, sauf de ma maman, la petite Olive belliqueuse

For my dad, Big Brave Ken, who isn't afraid of anything,
apart from my mum, Little Belligerent Olive.

Big Brave Brian copyright © Frances Lincoln Limited 2007
English text and illustrations copyright © M.P. Robertson 2007

French translation copyright © Frances Lincoln Limited 2008
Translation into French by ToLocalise
www.tolocalise.com
info@tolocalise.com

This edition published in Great Britain and in the USA in 2008 by
Frances Lincoln Children's Books, 4 Torriano Mews,
Torriano Avenue, London NW5 2RZ

www.franceslincoln.com

British Library Cataloguing in Publication Data available on request

ISBN 978-1-84507-886-7

The illustrations in this book are watercolour and black pen

Set in HooskerDont

Printed in Singapore

1 3 5 7 9 8 6 4 2

You can find out more about the books by M.P. Robertson
on his website: www.mprobertson.co.uk

CHRISTOPHE LE COSTAUD COURAGEUX

★

BIG BRAVE BRIAN

★

M.P. Robertson

F

FRANCES LINCOLN
CHILDREN'S BOOKS

Christophe le costaud courageux

est le gars le plus courageux du monde.

Big Brave Brian is the bravest man in the world.

Les gros ours gris grognons
qui vivent sous les escaliers
n'arrivent pas à la cheville de
Christophe le costaud courageux.

Grumpy Grizzly Bears
that live beneath the stairs
are no match for Big Brave Brian.

Christophe le costaud courageux n'a pas peur
des monstres de cabinet
croqueurs de fesses
qui hantent les toilettes.

Big Brave Brian is not afraid of

Bottom-Biting
Bog Monsters

that terrorize the toilet.

Les énormes araignées velues

Incy Wincy Spiders

qui grimpent à la gouttière n'effraient pas Christophe le costaud courageux.
that climb up the spout don't frighten Big Brave Brian.

Les limaces mangeuses de bave
qui boivent l'eau du bain comme de la soupe
ne font pas trembler Christophe.

Slime-Slurpin' Slug Creatures
that drink his bathwater like soup
hold no fear for Brian.

Les géants

répugnants qui le dévisagent
par la fenêtre de sa chambre
ne flanquent pas la frousse à Christophe.

Ghastly Gawping Giants

that stare through
his bedroom window
don't make Brian's
knees knock.

Les vilains lutins

dévoreurs d'ours
en peluche

qui dégringolent
du coffre à jouets
ne lui collent

pas une peur bleue.

Teddy Gobbling Goblins that tumble from the toy chest don't give Brian the collywobbles.

Les bruits insolites de la nuit

ne donnent pas la chair de poule à Christophe.

Things that go Bump in the Night don't give Brian the heebie-jeebies.

Les démons

grignoteurs de chaussettes
tapis sous le lit n'effraient pas
Christophe le costaud courageux.

Sock-Munching Demons
that lurk under the bed
don't scare Big Brave Brian.

Mais il y a une chose dont même
Christophe le
costaud courageux
a peur...

But there is one thing that even
Big Brave Brian
is scared of...

C'est de ranger sa chambre !

Cleaning his room!